Monster Goose Nursery Rhymes

By Henry, Josh, and Harrison Herz

Illustrated by Abigail Larson

PELICAN PUBLISHING COMPANY

GRETNA 2015

The word "Pelican" and the depiction of a pelican are
trademarks of Pelican Publishing Company, Inc., and are
registered in the U.S. Patent and Trademark Office.

Library of Congress Cataloging-in-Publication Data

Herz, Henry.
  Monster goose nursery rhymes / by Henry, Josh, and Harrison
Herz ; illustrated by Abigail Larson.
     pages cm
  ISBN 978-1-4556-2032-6 (hardcover : alk. paper) — ISBN 978-1-4556-
2033-3 (e-book) 1. Nursery rhymes, American. I. Herz, Josh. II.
Herz, Harrison. III. Larson, Abigail (Illustrator) IV. Title.
  PS3608.E7896M66 2015
  811'.6—dc23

                                                  2014028034

Printed in Malaysia
Published by Pelican Publishing Company, Inc.
1000 Burmaster Street, Gretna, Louisiana 70053

With gratitude to the Brothers Grimm, Gary Gygax,
my parents, and the Author of all things
—Henry Herz

HEFTY JACK HORNER
(to the tune of "Little Jack Horner")

Hefty Jack Horner
Sat in the corner,
Eating an elvish pie;
He put in his claw,
And pulled out a jaw,
And said, "What a
Good troll am I!"

LITTLE WITCH MUFFET

(to the tune of "Little Miss Muffet")

Little Witch Muffet
Sat on a tuffet,
Knowing not what to brew;
But when a big spider
Descended beside her,
She tossed it right into her stew.

ZOMBIE ROTTEN, QUITE FORGOTTEN
(to the tune of "Mary, Mary, Quite Contrary")

"Zombie rotten, quite forgotten,
How does your graveyard fare?"
"With skulls and bones for steppingstones,
It's enough to raise your hair."

ROAR, ROAR, OGRE.

(to the tune of "Baa, Baa, Black Sheep")

"Roar, roar, ogre,
Have you any gold?"
"Yes sir, yes sir, bags untold;
Some for the giants,
Some for the gnolls,
And some for the cunning dwarves
Who delve deep down holes."

HEY DOBLIN, DOBLIN
(to the tune of "Hey Diddle Diddle")

Hey doblin, doblin,
The gnome and the goblin,
The centaur ran through the lawn.
The minotaur laughed,
To see such sport,
And the imp ran away with the faun.

EENSY WEENSY BROWNIE

(to the tune of "Eensy Weensy Spider")

The eensy weensy brownie scaled up the palisade.
Down came a hail of arrows to dissuade.
Out came his shield
And blocked all of the darts.
And the eensy weensy brownie
Climbed up and stole some tarts.

WEE WILLIE WEREWOLF
(to the tune of "Wee Willie Winkie")

Wee Willie Werewolf runs through the street,
Looking for tardy children to eat;
Clawing at the window, sniffing at the lock,
Any children not in bed,
He will chase 'round the block.

EENIE, MEENIE, TINY? NO!
(to the tune of "Eenie, Meenie, Miney, Mo")

Eenie, meenie, tiny? No!
Catch an ettin by the toe.
If he hollers, let him go.
Eenie, meenie, tiny? No!

MARY HAD A HIPPOGRIFF

(to the tune of "Mary Had a Little Lamb")

Mary had a hippogriff,
Its feathers white as snow;
And everywhere that Mary went
The hippogriff did go.
It followed her to school one day,
Which was against the rule;
It made the children run away,
That hippogriff at school.

PETER, PETER, GOBLIN EATER
(to the tune of "Peter, Peter, Pumpkin Eater")

Peter, Peter, goblin eater,
Savored flavors that were sweeter;
He put fiends in a pumpkin shell,
And there he cooked them very well.

TAKE A LONG WALK

(to the tune of "Ride a Cock-Horse")

Take a long walk to Banbury Cross,
To see a green harpy upon a white horse.
Talons for fingers and claws on her toes,
She shall cause terror wherever she goes.

MANTICORE, MANTICORE
(to the tune of "Pussycat, Pussycat")

"Manticore, manticore,
Where did you go?"
"I went to Persia
To visit my foe."
"Manticore, manticore,
What did you there?"
"I conquered his castle
And made it my lair."

SING A SONG OF SIX SPRITES
(to the tune of "Sing a Song of Sixpence")

Sing a song of six sprites,
A forest full of dread;
Four-and-twenty pixies
Baked into bread!
When the loaf was opened,
It made a wondrous scene;
Wasn't that a fey whole wheat
To set before the queen?

THIS LITTLE HYDRA
(to the tune of "This Little Piggy")

This little hydra went to battle;
This little hydra did roam;
This little hydra had roast beef;
This little hydra had gnome;
And this little hydra went, "Hiss, hiss, hiss!"
All the way home.

APPENDIX (BESTIARY)

brownie (Scottish). Brownies are small humanoids that inhabit houses and at night help with the chores.

centaur (Greek). Centaurs have the head, arms, and torso of a human and the body and legs of a horse.

dwarf (Norse, German). Dwarves are small humanoids who live underground. They are known for their skill as smiths and miners, as well as their greed and stubbornness.

ettin (modern). Ettins are two-headed giants. The right head controls the right arm, and the left head the left arm. The heads sometimes bicker.

faun (Greek, Roman). Fauns are simple, forest-dwelling creatures with the head, arms, and torso of a human, two goat legs, and goat horns on their head.

giant (worldwide). Giants are immense and strong humanoids.

gnoll (modern). Gnolls are a cross between a gnome and a troll. Invented by Lord Dunsany in *The Book of Wonder,* they later appeared in Dungeons & Dragons as tall humanoid hyenas.

gnome (European). Gnomes are small, shy, and cunning humanoids who live underground and can move through earth as easily as humans move through air.

goblin (European). Goblins are small, evil humanoids and natural enemies of dwarves.

harpy (Greek, Roman). Harpies are evil, winged creatures with the head and upper torso of a woman and the wings, lower torso, and legs of an eagle.

hippogriff (Roman). Hippogriffs are intelligent, strong, fast-flying creatures, born from a mare and a griffin. They have the head, upper body, and wings of an eagle and the back legs of a horse.

hydra (Greek). Hydras are large, cave-dwelling, serpent-like beasts with many heads. Every time a head is cut off, two more grow in its place. It also has poisonous breath and blood.

imp (German). Imps are wild, lesser demons that often seek humans on whom to commit mischievous, not evil, acts.

manticore (Persian). Manticores are man-eating creatures with the body of a lion, human head (with three rows of sharp teeth), and sometimes horns or wings. They have a dragon or scorpion tail, from which they can shoot poisonous spines.

minotaur (Greek). Minotaurs are strong, man-eating creatures combining features from a bull and a human.

ogre (worldwide). Ogres are large, strong, dimwitted, and dangerous humanoids who eat humans.

pixie (Celtic). Pixies are small humanoids that live in underground ancestor sites. They are childlike and mischievous and don't like sprites.

sprite (worldwide). "Sprite" is a broad term for small spirits, such as elves or fairies, sometimes winged.

troll (Norse). Trolls are large, strong, dimwitted, and dangerous humanoids who live in caves. Sunlight turns trolls to stone.

werewolf (Greek, Roman). Werewolves are humans with the ability to shape-shift, at the appearance of a full moon, into an unnaturally strong and fast man-eating wolf.

witch (worldwide). Witches are women who cast magic spells, sometimes brew potions in cauldrons, and fly on broomsticks.

zombie (West Africa, Haiti). Zombies are evil, animated corpses hungry for human flesh or brains.